HUCKLEBERRY HILL
ELEMENTARY SCHOOL

One Green Apple

by Eve Bunting

Illustrated by Ted Lewin

Clarion Books
New York

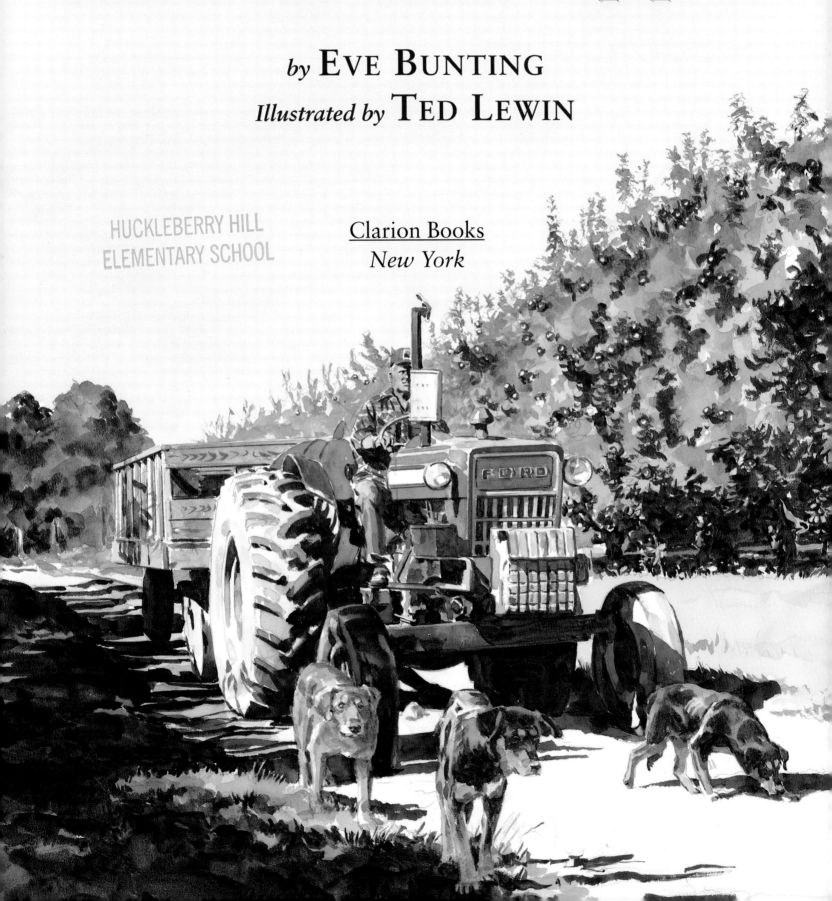

Clarion Books
a Houghton Mifflin Company imprint
215 Park Avenue South, New York, NY 10003
Text copyright © 2006 by Edward D. Bunting and Anne E. Bunting Family Trust
Illustrations copyright © 2006 by Ted Lewin Ltd.

The illustrations were executed in watercolor.
The text was set in 17-point Sabon.

Printed in Malaysia

Library of Congress Cataloging-in-Publication Data
Bunting, Eve, 1928–
One green apple / by Eve Bunting ; illustrated by Ted Lewin.
p. cm.
Summary: While on a school field trip to an orchard to make cider, a young
immigrant named Farah gains self-confidence when the green apple she
picks perfectly complements the other students' red apples.
ISBN 0-618-43477-1
[1. Self-confidence—Fiction. 2. Immigrants—Fiction. 3. Apples—Fiction.
4. School field trips—Fiction.] I. Lewin, Ted, ill. II. Title.
PZ7.B91527 One 2006
[E]—dc22   2005011378

ISBN-13: 978-0-618-43477-0   ISBN-10: 0-618-43477-1

TWP 10 9 8

4500287389

Once again, for Diana and her "apple cider kids." Thanks.
—E.B.

Thanks to Wilklow Orchards.
Special thanks to Samar Mahdi, my "Farah."
—T.L.

This is my second day in the new school in the new country.

There are to be no lessons today because we are going somewhere. Other days will not be like this one. Tomorrow I will go again to the class where I will learn to speak English.

Mothers drive us to the start of an orchard where a hay wagon is waiting. We climb on and lean against the bundles of hay. The wagon is pulled by a tractor and we jolt along. I think it odd to have boys and girls sit together. It was not like this in my village.

5

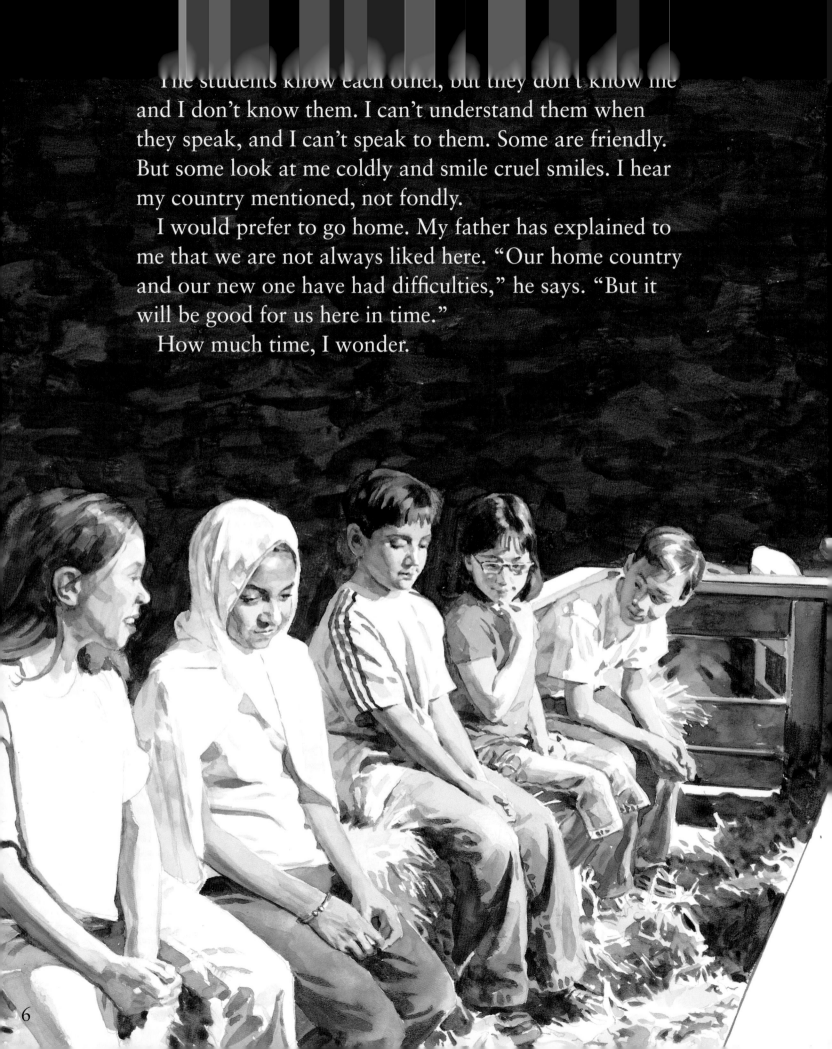

The students know each other, but they don't know me and I don't know them. I can't understand them when they speak, and I can't speak to them. Some are friendly. But some look at me coldly and smile cruel smiles. I hear my country mentioned, not fondly.

I would prefer to go home. My father has explained to me that we are not always liked here. "Our home country and our new one have had difficulties," he says. "But it will be good for us here in time."

How much time, I wonder.

I am different, too, in other ways. My jeans and T-shirt look like theirs, but my dupatta covers my head and shoulders. I have not seen anyone else wearing a dupatta, though all the girls and women in my home country do.

The girl who sits next to me smiles and points to herself. "Anna," she says. She points to me. "Farah!"

I nod and say, "Farah," which is my name. Then I look across the field where cows graze.

I am tight inside myself.

Three dogs come and run in front of us. I think they belong here and know the way.

I once had a dog called Haddis.

We stop at a place where apple trees bunch together. I find out we are to pick the fruit. Old apples have fallen in the grass. The three dogs are eating them,
crunch
crunch
crunch.
Their crunches sound like Haddis's.

11

Our teacher gathers us around her. She talks to the class. Then she looks at me in a kind way. "One," she says. She touches an apple, then picks it. "One," she says again. I am to take only one, as the other students have done. I nod. I want to say, "I understand. It's not that I am stupid. It is just that I am lost in this new place." But I don't know how to tell her.

I pull away from the rest. Beside me is a tree, shorter than the others, that does not seem to belong. It is small and alone, like me. A few hard green apples hang from its branches. I twist one off. It fits perfectly in my hand.

We hold our apples and run and slide down a hill. The dogs race ahead. Their ears blow backward, inside out, pink and shiny.

At the bottom of the hill is a little crooked house made of wood. I wonder if a cow lives in it, or a goat. Perhaps it is the home of a shepherd.

17

In the house is a wooden machine with a metal handle. I see no cow or goat or shepherd. The house is here for some other reason.

Our teacher lines us up. One by one we plop our apples into the machine. I will be last to drop my small green one. My teacher seems about to speak. Then she shrugs and smiles. A boy shouts, "Hey!" He moves toward me, as if to stop me from putting in my little green apple. But he is too late. It has already gone.

There are blades inside the machine that chop the apples,
ka-chunk
ka-chunk
ka-chunk.
The students begin to push on the handle. That presses the chopped-up apples.

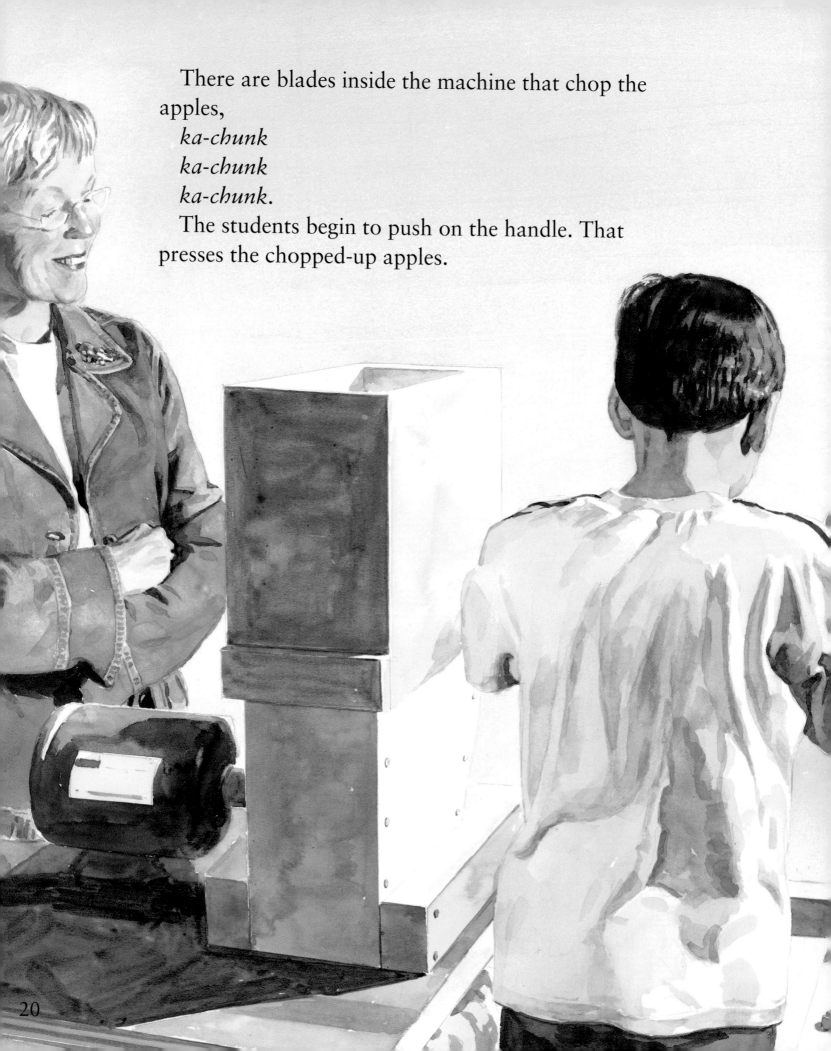

The skin and the pulp stay in the bag while the juice flows through.

I hang back, not sure if I should be with the others. Pushing the handle must be hard. They lean against it and grunt. I am strong. I can help. I take a step toward them.

Anna calls and waves to me to come beside her. A boy
makes a place for me on the handle between them.
I am pleased.

We push and push. It is hard, but we are working together and we can do it.
The juice drips down,
drip
drip
drip.

Our teacher has brought paper cups. We line up again, fill them, and drink. We lick our lips. I think I taste my special apple.

"Apple cider," Anna says. That must be what we are drinking. I say the word inside myself, where it can't be heard, "*App-ell*." The other word is too difficult.

Our teacher is speaking. She is holding out a bag for our cups and making signs that we must get ready to leave.

Anna sits next to me in the wagon as we ride back.
There is a boy on my other side. "Jim," he says and points
at himself.

I nod. "Jim," I say silently.

Hay tickles my arms and makes Anna sneeze. It smells
of dry sunshine.

Jim pats his stomach, and a belch jumps from his throat. Everyone laughs. I do, too.

Laughs sound the same as at home. Just the same. So do sneezes and belches and lots of things. It is the words that are strange. But soon I will know their words. I will blend with the others the way my apple blended with the cider.

I take a deep breath.

"App-ell," I say.
Anna claps.
I smile
and smile
and smile.

It is my first outside-myself word.
There will be more.